My Magic Wand

GROWING WITH THE SEASONS

Poems by
Pat Mora

Pictures by
Amber Alvarez

Lee & Low Books Inc. *New York*

My thanks to my supportive editor Louise May; to the talented illustrator Amber Alvarez; and in memory of Tom Low —P.M.

Edited by Louise E. May · Designed by Abby Dening
Production by The Kids at Our House
The text is set in KG Primary Penmanship
The illustrations are rendered in colored pencil, loose ground pigment, calligraphy ink, watercolor, oil pastel, and marker, enhanced with a little bit of computer magic.
Manufactured in China by Jade Productions
Printed on paper from responsible sources
10 9 8 7 6 5 4 3 2 1
First Edition

Library of Congress Cataloging-in-Publication Data
Names: Mora, Pat, author. | Alvarez, Amber, illustrator.
Title: My magic wand : growing with the seasons / poems by Pat Mora ; pictures by Amber Alvarez.
Description: First edition. | New York : Lee & Low Books Inc., [2021] | Summary: "A collection of original poems that celebrate family, universal childhood experiences, and the pure pleasure a young girl feels as her mastery and understanding grow throughout the seasons of a year" —Provided by publisher.
Identifiers: LCCN 2020027135 | ISBN 9781643790855 (hardcover) ISBN 9781643794693 (epub)
Subjects: LCSH: Seasons—Juvenile poetry. | Growth—Juvenile poetry. | Mexican Americans—Juvenile poetry. | Children's poetry, American.
Classification: LCC PS3563.O73 M87 2021 | DDC 811/.54—dc23
LC record available at https://lccn.loc.gov/2020027135

With love to my spunky granddaughter, Bonny
—P.M.

For my brilliant grandmothers, Betty Bryner
and Adele Flores; your stars light my way.
—A.A.

My Magic Wand

I can say my ABCs.
I can write them too.
My pencil is my magic wand.
I'm five, and made my songs for you,
　　for you.
I made my songs for you.

I Can Fly

Watch me fly
    on my new red sled. I slide
      down the slope
        on smooth snow
my tongue tasting
    flakes of winter's white cold.

Speaking Spanish

We fly from the snow to Mexico.
We fly from white cold to warm
    sun and sand.

I say, *"Buenos días,*
gracias, buenas noches."

We see the huge sea
and smell the salty breeze.

We run across the hot sand
into the waves that chase our toes.

At the market, I choose
a white dress
and help an artist make me
a blue bracelet and ring.

I spin to Mexican music,
and Dad and I eat yummy
mango ice cream.

Near the sea,
we are the happy three.

Turtle Time

Slowly I walk with a basin
of wet sand and three little green
sea turtles, *tortugas*. I pour
the turtles near the shore.

They scurry, scurry
on their little flippers into
soft waves that carry the turtles
into their new wet home.

The Artist

The spring sun warms my art table.
It is heaped
    with treasures, *tesoros*—
plain paper and fancy paper,
    beads and string to make jewelry,
markers, paint, glitter,
    and glue for my sparkling gems—
a rainbow of fun.

    I'm a happy artist!

Growing a Garden of Colors

By our yellow daffodils
and orange tulips—

I help Mom plant
purple pansies,
white daisies,
red snapdragons,
and pink primroses,

a garden of colors, *colores*,
and sweet scents
for ladybugs, butterflies,
hummingbirds, lizards,
     and me.

Let's Dance!

Watch us dance!

A little ballet,
some jazzy steps,
and country swings,
then hip-hopping
and line dancing.

Now we'll do them again.
¡A bailar!
Come join our spin!

Becoming a Fish

I put my toes in—
splish, splash.

Cito holds my hands,
walks in the pool,
and I kick my feet.

I hold my breath and put
my face in the cool blue ripples.

With Mom's arms under me,
I float on my back,
and the water holds me too.

I splash, play, and float.
A nice man says, "You are a fish!"

Yes. I am a slithery summer fish,
a *pececita.*

Delicious!

Cita and I read the recipe.
We measure and stir
to make sweet dough.
With cookie cutters,
I shape flowers, moons, stars.

Slowly they bake, and our house
smells like a giant cookie.

Yum-m-m! Delicious!

New Friend

Wearing my new cowgirl boots,
I visit a horse, a *caballo*, named Texas.
    I look at him, and he looks at me
        with his big brown eyes.

He lets me gently brush his muzzle.

His owner gives me a riding helmet
and helps me climb on.
    I hold the reins.

I am so high! Texas takes me for a ride.

After I climb down,
I feed Texas some treats.
    I look at him, and he looks at me
        with his big brown eyes.

I brush him softly and hum a little song.

I Wonder

How do cactus grow their spines?
Don't babies get tired of just sleeping
and sleeping?
Why doesn't my friend, my *amiga*,
want to hold my hand?
Doesn't a giraffe get tired of looking
down, down, down?
How do ladybugs grow their black spots?
Where do candy makers hide
their tasty mountains of sugar?

A Celebration

What a table!

At my friend's house,
Mom and I see
the strawberry cake
Vivian's dad made
and a bowl of pink frosting,
candies, and tiny, shiny, silver balls.

We share and decorate the cake.
I say "please" and "thank you."
Vivian is smiling. She tells us
to blow our paper horns.

She carries Curly, her snail
that died, to a shady place,
and we put some leaves
like a blanket over Curly.

I start us singing,
"This is the place Curly will rest,
Curly will rest,
Curly will rest.
This is the place Curly will rest,
under the pretty tree."

Walking home, I say,
"At school, the fish had babies.
We're studying the cycle of life."

The Best

Today, I can take care of you, Moosie.

Fresh water in your bowl.
    Slurp, slurp, slurp!

Food to help you grow.
    Munch, munch, munch!

Your leash for our walk.
Whoa! No flying for you and me, Moosie.

Time for more water and rest.
I'll pat you in your cozy nest.

I'll say, "My Moosie is the best!
My big old Moosie is the best!"

A Singing Ring

Candles twinkle on my cake.
I shine inside too.

In a ring, my friends and family sing,
"Happy birthday to you,
happy birthday to you!"

Whoosh! I blow out six candles.

My face a big smile,
    I am all shiny inside.

I feel like I swallowed a star.

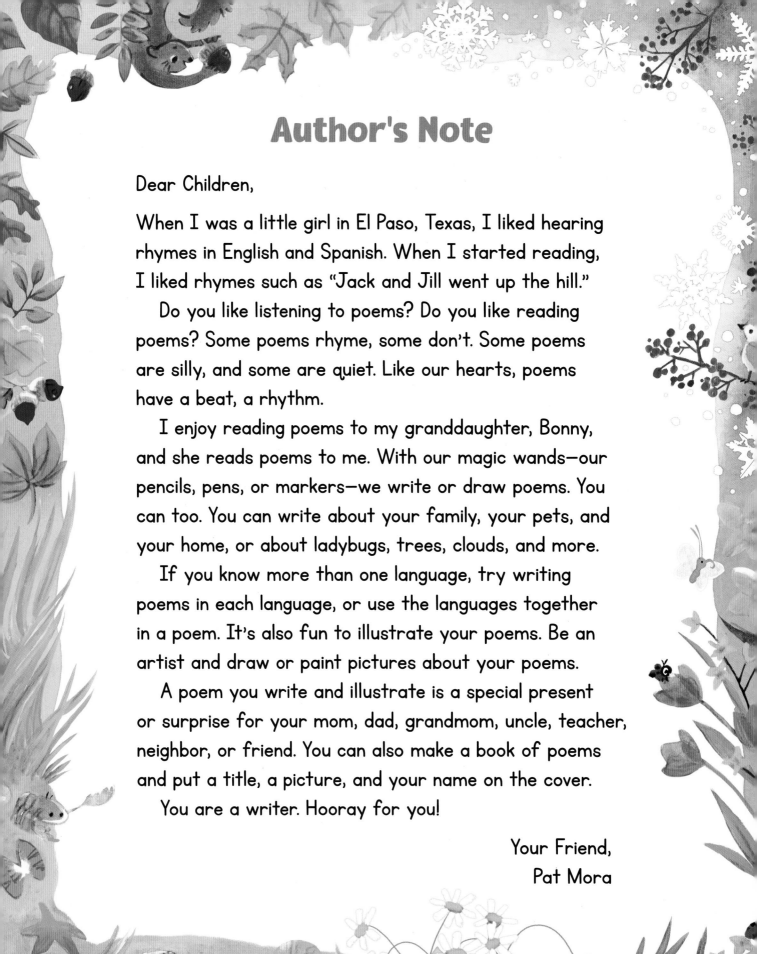

Author's Note

Dear Children,

When I was a little girl in El Paso, Texas, I liked hearing rhymes in English and Spanish. When I started reading, I liked rhymes such as "Jack and Jill went up the hill."

Do you like listening to poems? Do you like reading poems? Some poems rhyme, some don't. Some poems are silly, and some are quiet. Like our hearts, poems have a beat, a rhythm.

I enjoy reading poems to my granddaughter, Bonny, and she reads poems to me. With our magic wands—our pencils, pens, or markers—we write or draw poems. You can too. You can write about your family, your pets, and your home, or about ladybugs, trees, clouds, and more.

If you know more than one language, try writing poems in each language, or use the languages together in a poem. It's also fun to illustrate your poems. Be an artist and draw or paint pictures about your poems.

A poem you write and illustrate is a special present or surprise for your mom, dad, grandmom, uncle, teacher, neighbor, or friend. You can also make a book of poems and put a title, a picture, and your name on the cover.

You are a writer. Hooray for you!

Your Friend,
Pat Mora